Charles M. Schulz

Sally's Christmas Miracle

HarperFestival®

A Division of HarperCollinsPublishers

HarperCollins®, 🎬®, and HarperFestival® are trademarks
of HarperCollins Publishers, Inc.
Conceived and produced by Packaged Goods Incorporated,
276 Fifth Avenue, New York, NY 10001. A Quarto Company.
A Packaged Goods Incorporated Book
Copyright © 1996 by United Feature Syndicate, Inc.
PEANUTS © United Feature Syndicate, Inc.
Based on the PEANUTS® comic strip by Charles M. Schulz.

Library of Congress Cataloging-in-Publication Data
Schulz, Charles M.
   Sally's Christmas miracle / by Charles M. Schulz
      p.   cm.
   Summary: Trouble ensues when Charlie Brown's little sister, Sally, "falls
down" a Christmas tree in her neighbor's yard and the kid next door wants
it back.
   ISBN 0-694-00899-0—ISBN 0-06-027448-4 (lib. bdg.)
   [1. Christmas trees—Fiction.   2. Christmas—Fiction.]   I. Title.
PZ7.S38877Sal   1996   95-26453
[E]—dc20   CIP
                                                        AC

"I don't know how to cut down
a Christmas tree."

"When I look at it, I hope it'll just fall down."

"Hey, kid, what're you doin' in our yard?! You weren't thinkin' of cuttin' that tree down, were ya?"

"I don't know
how to cut
a tree down.
What if it
just falls
down?"

"Hey, kid, you got a sister or something with yellow hair? She stole a Christmas tree from our yard."

"I didn't steal it. He said if it fell over, I could have it. When I looked at it, it fell over. It was a Christmas miracle!"

“What are you standing on
our porch for? Go home!”

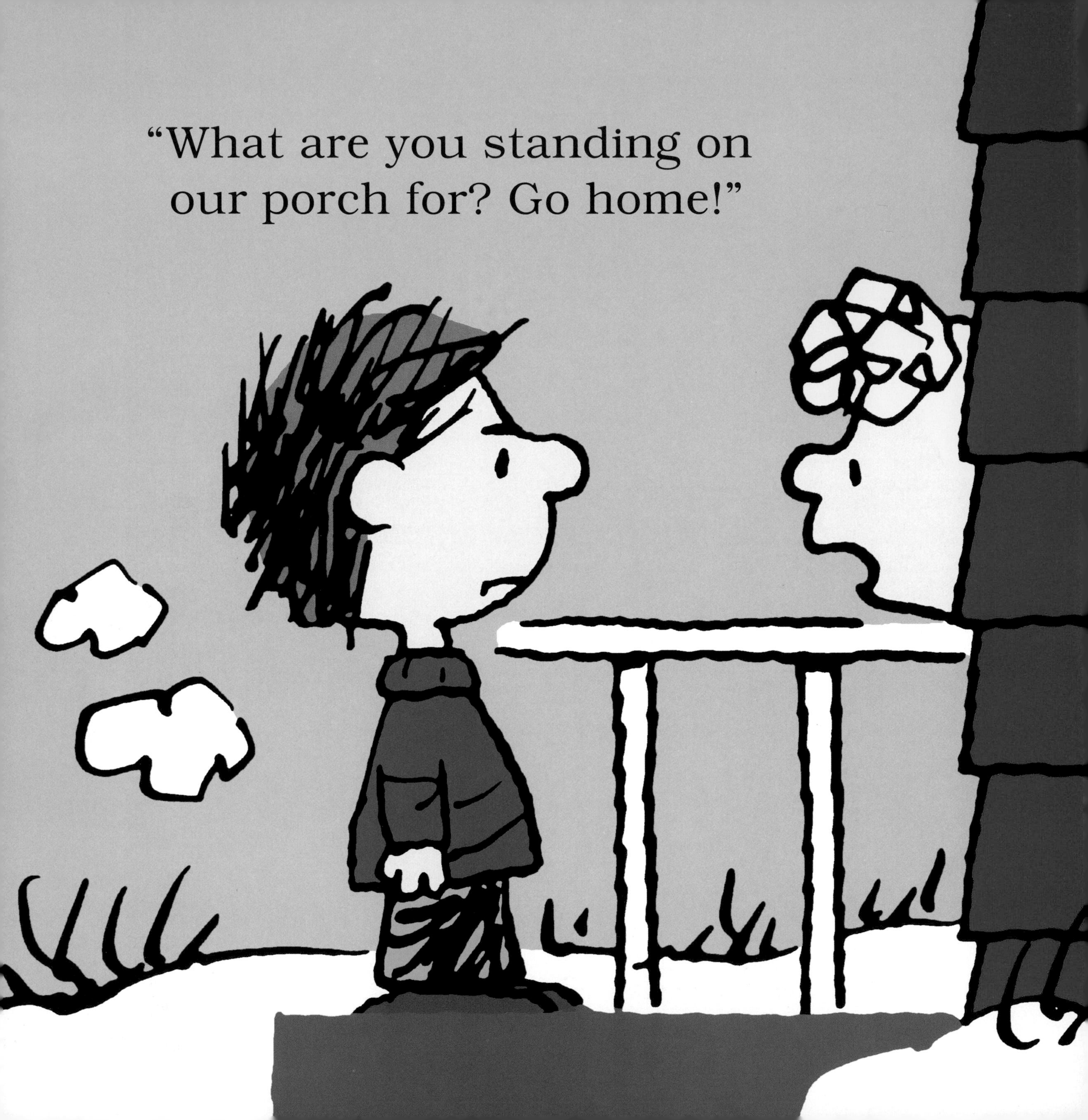

"Now, get off our porch, or
I'll call the dog!"

"I can't sleep, big brother.
Do you think I should give the
tree back to that ugly kid?"

"Why?" asked Charlie Brown.
"Are you starting to feel guilty?"

"No! He said I could have the
tree if it fell over. I don't feel
guilty at all!"

"Tomorrow is Christmas Eve."

"Now I feel guilty."

"No, keep it! I was wrong.
It's yours! I said if it fell
over, it was yours. Keep it!"